ELISA KLEVEN

A Monster in the House

Dutton Children's Books • New York

Library of Congress Cataloging-in-Publication Data

Kleven, Elisa.

A monster in the house/by Elisa Kleven.—1st ed.   p.   cm.

Summary: A boy listens to his new neighbor describe the monster

that lives in her house, who screams when awakened,

yells for food, spits up on everything, and sucks his toes.

ISBN 0-525-45973-1

[1. Babies—Fiction.   2. Monsters—Fiction.]

I. Title.

PZ7.K6783875Mo   1998   [E]—dc21   98-5250   CIP   AC

Published in the United States 1998 by Dutton Children's Books,

a division of Penguin Putnam Books for Young Readers

375 Hudson Street, New York, New York 10014

Designed by Sara Reynolds

Printed in Hong Kong

First Edition

1 3 5 7 9 10 8 6 4 2

FOR HELEN, KATHLEEN, SHERRY,
MIA, AND BEN

He lives there all the time. He's never going away. He gets mad if we don't pay attention to him every single second!

Don't your parents protect you from him?

No, they give him whatever he wants. They talk to him in their sweetest voices, even when he wakes us all up at night, yelling as loud as he can.

What does he yell for?

For monster food!

Monster food! Does he eat kids?

No, just special monster milk—
and smushed-up bananas with
mashed-up prunes and smashed
split peas with soggy squash
and mushy cereal.

Yuck!
What a gross monster!
What else does he do?

VITAMIN M

CERTIFIED IMPURE
MONSTER MILK
3 GALLONS

He smears his food, like finger paint,
on everything he touches.
He rubs it on his hands like soap
and squeezes it through his fingers.

Pudding jiggles on his nose!
Egg yolk dribbles through his toes!

Ugh—what a messy monster!

The messiest in the world.
You know what else? After he eats,
he spits up lots of slimy,
sticky food.

Spits it up!

On everyone. And everything.
The rugs, the beds, the couch,
the house. His brand-new clothes.
My nicest shoes. Mom's prettiest
dresses. Dad's shirts. He'd spit
up on the president if he could!

Oh, my gosh.
What a rude monster!
Does he say bad words, too?

He says "Grrr-gaah-ir-oogh-dah-bizzzh-arrgh!" and gurgles and burps, and drools and drips, and makes sloppy, gloppy, goopy, poopy messes on himself.

Isn't he embarrassed?

Nothing embarrasses him! He just lies there sucking on his toes while Mom or Dad cleans him up.

He sucks on his toes?

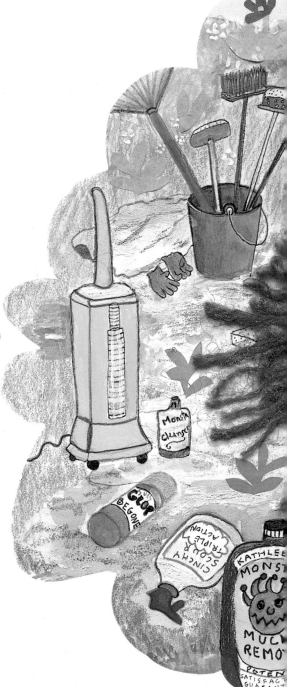

And he sucks on his fingers—
and on my fingers, too. Once
he tried to suck on my nose. He
sucks on blankets, books, and
balls. He sucks on all his toys.

His toys?
So what does he play with?

He likes to play with wrapping paper more than the presents inside. He likes to bang his spoon and plate, and crumple our mail, and yank the cat's tail, and grab at Mom's glasses and tug on Dad's tie.

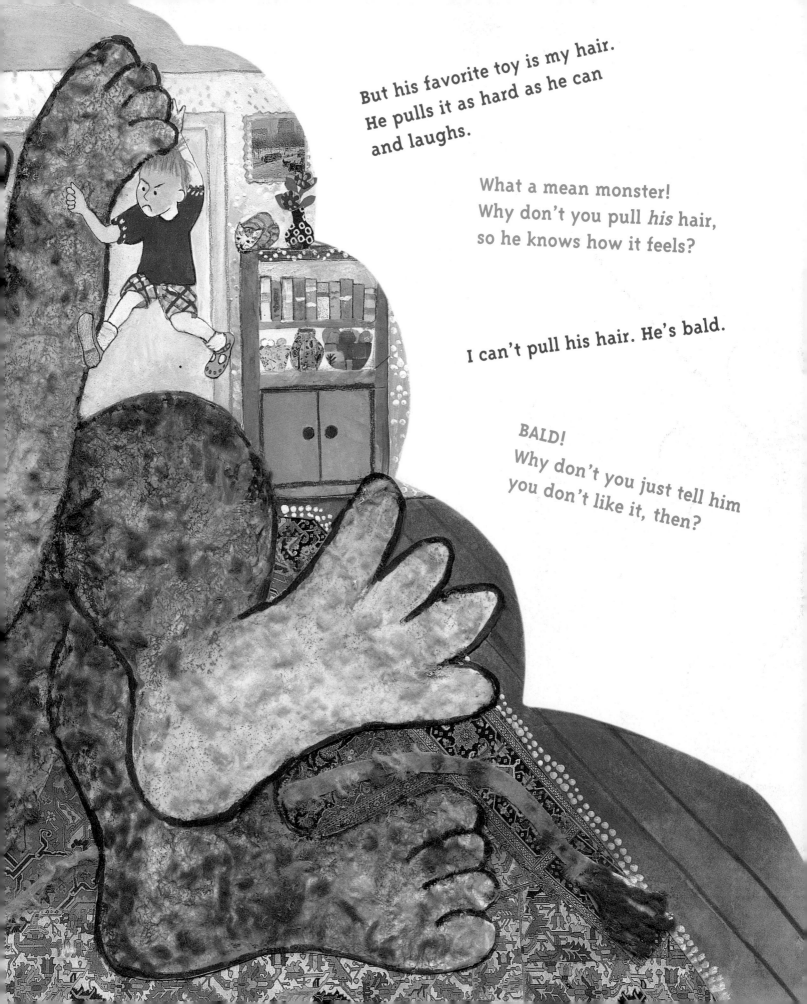

But his favorite toy is my hair.
He pulls it as hard as he can
and laughs.

What a mean monster!
Why don't you pull *his* hair,
so he knows how it feels?

I can't pull his hair. He's bald.

BALD!
Why don't you just tell him
you don't like it, then?

Because he's too little to understand.

He's little?

Little. And soft.

If he's so little and soft, then why don't you just chase him away?

It wouldn't do any good—
he can't run. He can't even walk.

This monster can't walk?

Don't worry—he loves to be carried! And cuddled and snuggled and kissed on his belly after his bath, when he smells like fresh warm bread.

Monsters don't smell like fresh warm bread!

Mine does.
And I love it when he smiles.

What makes him smile?

I do!
Want to see?
I think he's awake.

It's only your baby brother.
I *knew* you didn't have
a monster in your house!

Yikes! I'm glad
he missed my shoe!

Think he'd like to
play monster with me?

Sure. He's good at it.
Let's take him out
in his monstermobile.

Sweetie, stop calling your brother a monster. You were just like him when you were a baby, you know!

Weren't we all.

There you go, Monster Guy.

Not me.
I was way worse!

Cool! Argh.

Grr. Gaah-ir-oogh-grrr.

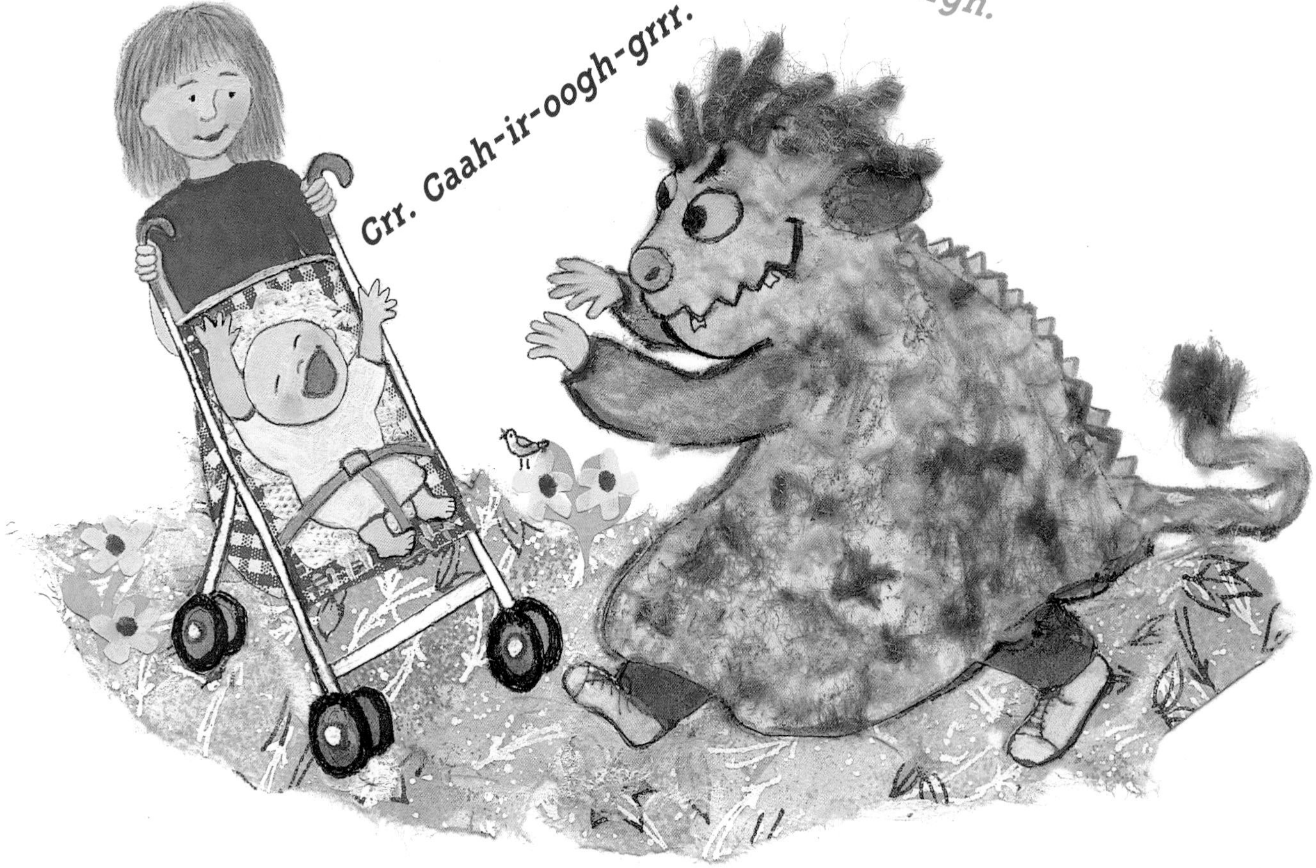